THE
CHRISTMAS TREE
WHO LOVED
TRAINS

THE CHRISTMAS

ANNIE SILVESTRO

ILLUSTRATED BY
PAOLA ZAKIMI

HARPER
An Imprint of HarperCollinsPublishers

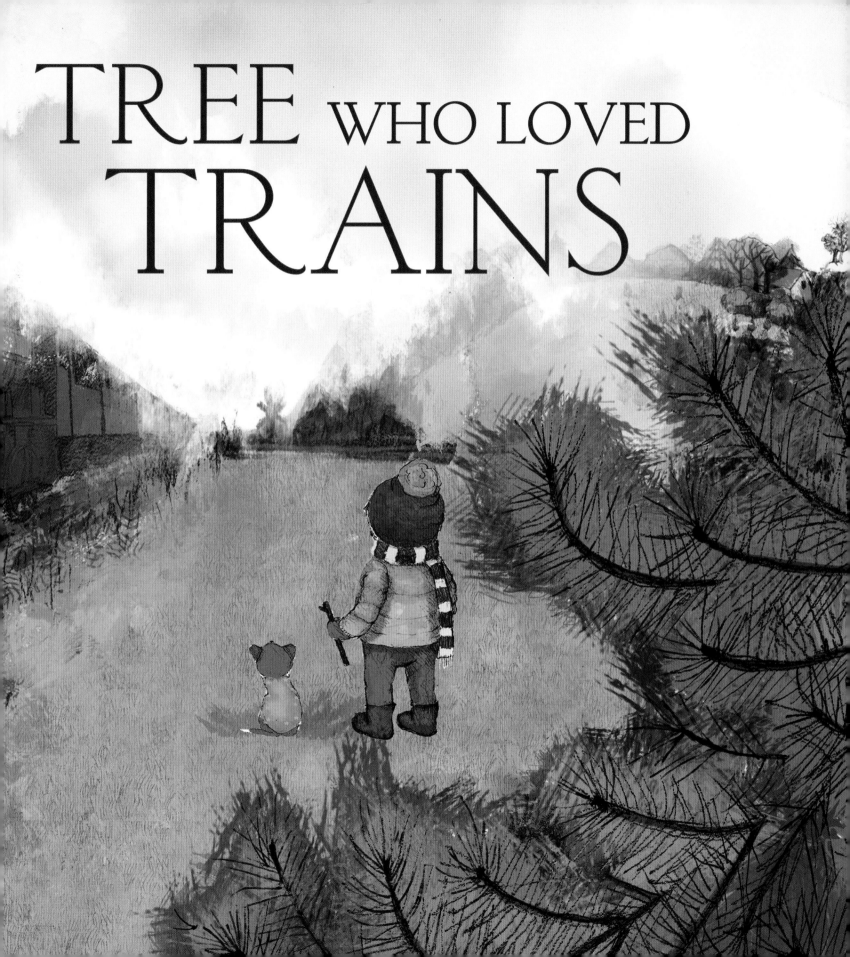

TREE WHO LOVED
TRAINS

For Sam, the boy who loves trains

—A.S.

For Sei

—P.Z.

The Christmas Tree Who Loved Trains
Text copyright © 2018 by Annie Silvestro
Illustrations copyright © 2018 by Paola Zakimi
All rights reserved. Manufactured in China.
No part of this book may be used or reproduced in any manner whatsoever without
written permission except in the case of brief quotations embodied in critical articles
and reviews. For information address HarperCollins Children's Books, a division of
HarperCollins Publishers, 195 Broadway, New York, NY 10007.
www.harpercollinschildrens.com

Library of Congress Control Number: 2017954032
ISBN 978-0-06-256168-8

The artist used pencil and Adobe Photoshop to create the digital illustrations for this book.
Typography by Chelsea C. Donaldson
18 19 20 21 22 SCP 10 9 8 7 6 5 4 3 2 1
❖
First Edition

A pine tree grew in the farthest corner of the tree farm.
She sat alone on a small patch of land that bordered the
train track.

The tree loved the trains—their speed, their click-clacking wheels, their powerful engines.

When she heard one rumbling in the distance, the
tree would stand tall, her needles tingling, then . . .

ZOOM!

Her branches would ripple in the wind as the train roared past. The noise kept birds from nesting in her branches and squirrels from playing nearby, but the tree didn't mind—the trains were company enough.

One morning a little boy ran all the way to the
farthest corner of the tree farm. He planned to pick
a Christmas tree, but first he hoped to see a train.

He watched the track.
He waited.

Then . . . *ZOOM!*

His hair rippled in the wind as the
train roared past.

The boy smiled. He noticed the tree.
She seemed to be smiling, too.
"This is the one, Dad," he said.

Soon a truck came to dig the tree out of the ground.
Workers bound her roots in a burlap sack.
The man and the boy strapped her onto their pickup
and drove away.

The tree could no longer hear the trains.
She could no longer feel them blasting past.
She no longer stood tall, either.

When they got home, the man carried
the tree inside.
    He shuffled her into the corner of a room.
    It felt strange. Dark. Cramped.
    The tree missed *her* corner.
    She missed being outside.
    Most of all, she missed the trains.
    At night, when the house was silent,
she imagined she heard their whistles.

One day the man strung lights around her. The family hung
objects from her branches. When they finished, the boy placed
a star on her topmost branch.

The tree fell asleep to the ringing of sleigh bells.
She dreamed of trains.

As she slept, she didn't notice the whoosh from the chimney.
She didn't hear the boots gliding swiftly across the floor.
She didn't feel the rustling under her branches.

When she woke, it was to the sound of happy squeals.
She heard something else, too; a noise that had her
needles tingling once again.
Could it be?

It was!
A train chugged along its track right beneath her.

The tree twinkled.
She carried her lights and ornaments proudly.

The boy played around the Christmas tree
all morning long and for days after.
The tree had never been happier.
It was a joyous season.

Too soon the man packed up
the ornaments, the lights, the star.
Finally, he put away the train.
The tree grew anxious.

"Don't worry," whispered the boy. "We've found
the perfect spot for you."

The man lifted her onto his pickup.
The boy jumped in beside her.
They traveled down a dusty road.
Past a barn.
A chicken coop.
A scarecrow.
That's when she heard it.

CHUGGA

The tree stretched to see.

CHUGGA

The pickup came to a stop.

CHOO CHOO

As the tree stretched upright, she felt the

ZOOM!

It was even better than she rembered.

The man and the boy planted the tree at the edge of their farm.
There, she still loves the trains—their speed, their click-clacking wheels, their powerful engines.
Her branches ripple as they pass.
Birds and squirrels stay away, but the tree doesn't mind.
She has the trains to keep her company.

And even better, the little boy.